Tony Bradman
Happy Ever After
SAVE the FOREST!
THE UGLY DUCKLING RETURNS
Illustrated by Sarah Warburton
ORCHARD BOOKS

"Can you see him yet?" said one of the gaggle of giggling goose girls hanging around outside Forest TV. They were being held back by a line of security guards. "I think I'll die if he doesn't come soon..."

EEEEEK!
THERE HE IS!
AUTO GRAPHS

An elegant figure had appeared at the studio door. Soon all the goose girls were screaming with excitement and waving and calling out. Even the security guards were looking over their shoulders, their mouths open in wonder.

“Give us a smile, Swan!” yelled a troll with a camera. A crowd of reporters had appeared, pushing and shoving each other and taking lots of pictures.

"Of course," said the elegant figure, and smiled. Hundreds of camera flashes went off…

…and several of the goose girls swooned in complete ecstasy.

The elegant figure laughed, climbed into his limo, and was swept away. He relaxed in the luxurious leather seat and shook his head in amazement.

How strange it was to have crowds waiting everywhere he went, and to hear them calling him 'Swan'. After all, he still thought of himself by the name he had been given when he had first hatched out of his egg – the Ugly Duckling.

Life had certainly changed for him since those days. Everybody had been horrible to him then.

They had made fun of his big head…

…and his stubby brown feathers and his clumsy walk.

But he had grown up to be a beautiful swan. In fact, he had turned out to be so good looking he had become a model, and now he was the biggest celebrity in the Forest.

He appeared on TV, and his picture was in all the magazines.

Things were good for the Ugly Duckling, and he hoped they were going to stay that way. He would hate going back to being the way he had been before...

Suddenly he realised the limo had stopped. He looked out of the window, and saw they were in a line of cars. "What's the problem, driver?" he said.

"Too many cars, that's what," muttered the driver, honking the limo's horn – HONK! "The traffic in the Forest is terrible, and it's getting worse every day."

Now the Ugly Duckling felt depressed, and also a little guilty. Life might be good for him, but there was a lot wrong with the world.

His driver was right. There was far too much traffic in the Forest, and the pollution was awful.

Nobody seemed to care, though, and that worried the Ugly Duckling. By the time he finally got home to his fabulous mansion hours later, he had decided he wanted to do something about it. But what?

He leafed through the local paper, brooding. A tiny item caught his attention...

Some people had started a new anti-pollution campaign called *Save The Forest!* They were planning to have a rally the very next day, and the Ugly Duckling decided he would go along.

He disguised himself so he wouldn't attract attention, and stood at the back of the crowd. After he'd listened to all the speeches he went up to Rapunzel, who was one of the organisers.

"Oh, er...hi," he said. "I was wondering if I could do anything to help?"

"Yes, please. We could always use another volunteer to hand out leaflets," said Rapunzel.

Then she paused, and peered at him a little more closely. "Hang on," she murmured, her eyes growing wide. "I don't believe it..."

The Ugly Duckling's heart sank, but he needn't have worried. The other organisers recognised him too, but they were all just pleased to meet him. They got talking, and at last the Ugly Duckling asked how the campaign was going.

"Not very well so far," Rapunzel said gloomily. The others nodded. "We can't seem to get any real publicity. Forest TV told us we're not exciting enough."

Suddenly the Ugly Duckling had an idea. "Maybe I could have a word with them," he said. "They're always asking me if I want to do something special."

"Could you really?" said Rapunzel. "That would be absolutely wonderful."

The Ugly Duckling went to see his contacts at Forest TV the very next day.

He told them about how important the *Save The Forest!* campaign was, and explained that he wanted to help his new friends get lots of publicity.

He had agreed to speak at their next rally, and hoped that Forest TV would cover it. The Forest TV trolls seemed very excited and promised they would, but the Ugly Duckling didn't stop there.

He visited all the newspapers and magazines in the Forest, and made them promise to send their reporters to the rally as well.

That evening, he cycled over to see Rapunzel in her palace. He had given up being driven around in a limo now he'd realised it was bad for the Forest.

"Wow, that's great!" said Rapunzel when the Ugly Duckling told her what he had done. "We'll have to make sure there are plenty of leaflets and posters."

Rapunzel and her team worked very hard for the next couple of days, getting everything ready for the rally. They hired a hall in the centre of the Forest and set up stalls where people could get information or volunteer for the campaign.

And at the far end of the hall was a stage for people to stand on to make speeches.

The Ugly Duckling stood in the wings waiting for the rally to begin. He was scheduled to make the first speech, and he was feeling happy and rather excited.

At last they opened the doors – and a huge crowd stampeded in, trampling over the stalls in a wild rush to get to the stage. There were TV trolls, dozens of reporters, and lots of fans, including the usual gaggle of giggling goose girls.

SWAN! SWAN!
I ♥ SWAN

"Give us a smile, Swan!" the reporters yelled, pushing and shoving each other. It was a complete disaster…and the Ugly Duckling was horrified.

"I'm sorry, Rapunzel," he said later, when they were tidying up the hall. "I don't seem to have been much help after all. Quite the opposite, in fact."

“Well, thanks for trying,” Rapunzel said sadly. “I suppose we’ll just have to keep thinking. There must be some way we can get our message across…”

That night, the Ugly Duckling sat watching TV in his mansion and brooding again. He felt really fed up. Once upon a time he had desperately wanted to be beautiful. But now it seemed that being good looking wasn't any use at all.

Nobody had been interested in what he wanted to say – the reporters and fans had only cared about what he looked like. So the campaign still wasn't getting any publicity, and that meant the Forest was becoming more polluted every day.

Suddenly he sat up. Maybe he could shock everyone into seeing things differently! He thought about it – then called Rapunzel and told her his plan.

"I like it!" said Rapunzel, and laughed. "If that doesn't work, nothing will!"

A few days later she announced that *Save The Forest!* would be holding another rally, and that Swan would be there.

TV crews and reporters and fans flocked to the same hall, but this time the curtains were drawn across the stage.

And when they were pulled back, they revealed…not Swan, but the Ugly Duckling!

It had taken a lot of effort with make-up and false feathers, but he had managed to make himself appear like his old self. Everybody gasped.

"This is the way I used to look," he said. "But we're making the Forest look just as ugly because of all the pollution we create. We can't go on ignoring it."

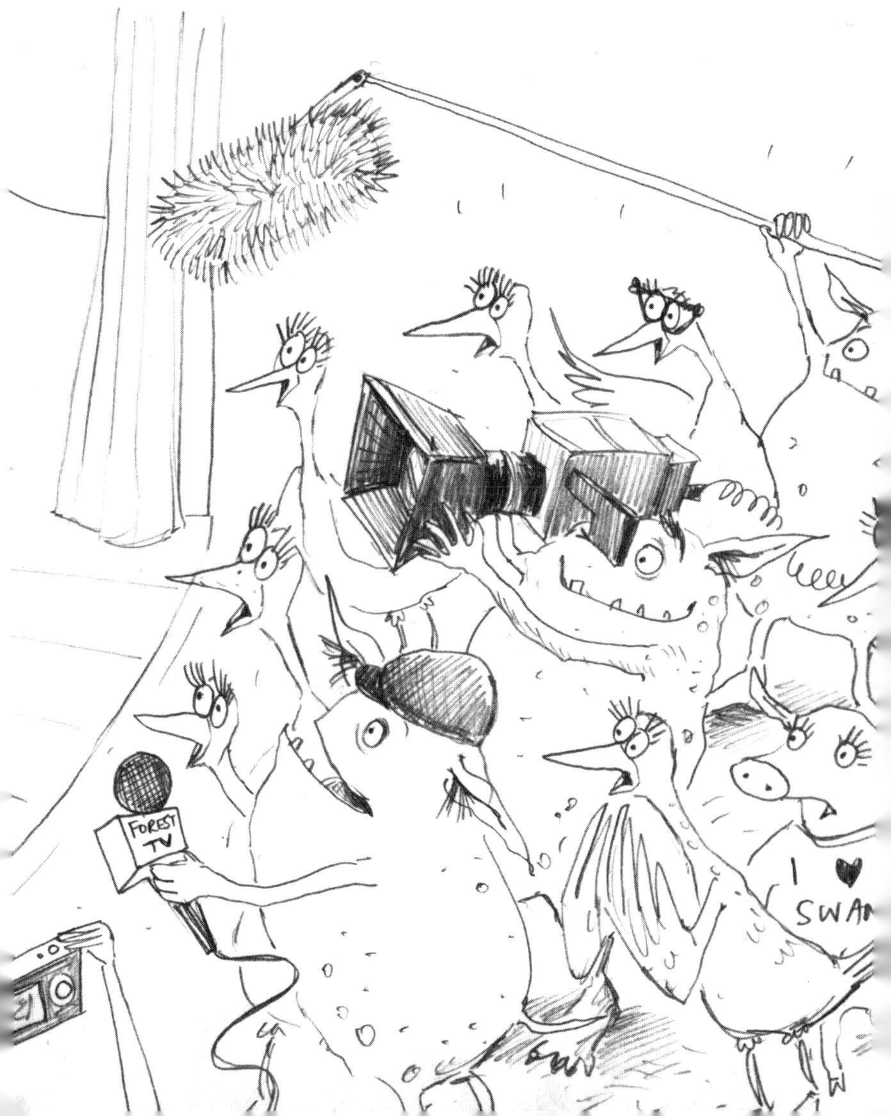

It was a triumph, of course.

Everybody listened to his speech, and to lots of other speeches, and the *Save The Forest!* campaign got the publicity it needed.

The Ugly Duckling soon went back to being Swan, and the gaggle of goose girls still swooned when he smiled. But he decided he could live with that.

Because of the Ugly Duckling, everyone in the Forest joined the *Save The Forest!* campaign and lived…

HAPPILY EVER AFTER!